RATNiP
Right on Your Tail!

BY **CAM HIGGINS** • ILLUSTRATED BY **ALLISON STEINFELD**

LITTLE SIMON
New York Amsterdam/Antwerp London
Toronto Sydney/Melbourne New Delhi

This book is a work of fiction. Any references to historical events, real people, or real places are used fictitiously. Other names, characters, places, and events are products of the author's imagination, and any resemblance to actual events or places or persons, living or dead, is entirely coincidental.

LITTLE SIMON
An imprint of Simon & Schuster Children's Publishing Division
1230 Avenue of the Americas, New York, New York 10020
First Little Simon hardcover edition May 2025
© 2025 by Simon & Schuster, LLC
Also available in a Little Simon paperback edition.
All rights reserved, including the right of reproduction in whole or in part in any form.
LITTLE SIMON is a registered trademark of Simon & Schuster, LLC, and associated colophon is a trademark of Simon & Schuster, LLC.
RATNIP is a trademark of Simon & Schuster, LLC.
For information about special discounts for bulk purchases, please contact Simon & Schuster Special Sales at 1-866-506-1949 or business@simonandschuster.com.
The Simon & Schuster Speakers Bureau can bring authors to your live event. For more information or to book an event contact the Simon & Schuster Speakers Bureau at 1-866-248-3049 or visit our website at www.simonspeakers.com.
Book design by Brittany Fetcho
Manufactured in the United States of America 0425 LAK
2 4 6 8 10 9 7 5 3 1
CIP data for this book is available from the Library of Congress.
ISBN 9781665963527 (hc)
ISBN 9781665963510 (pbk)
ISBN 9781665963534 (ebook)

Contents

CHAPTER 1: Dodge the Trash — 1

CHAPTER 2: Eye on the Prize — 13

CHAPTER 3: Gym Rats — 23

CHAPTER 4: Not-So-Easy Workout — 37

CHAPTER 5: In It to Win it — 49

CHAPTER 6: The Race Is On! — 59

CHAPTER 7: Run, Run, Run — 73

CHAPTER 8: Wrong Way — 85

CHAPTER 9: The Final Obstacle — 97

CHAPTER 10: And the Winner Is . . . — 109

CHAPTER 1
DODGE THE TRASH

It was a very windy night in The City. The branches shook, and the windowpanes rattled in the pizza parlor where I lived with my family.

I don't know about you, but I love windy nights. That's because I get to play one of my favorite games, Dodge the Trash!

The rules of the game are simple: Don't get hit by any of the trash that flies your way!

I stepped outside onto the sidewalk with my brothers, Pepperoni and Veggie.

We got into position, crouching low to the ground. Our fur stood straight up, our ears were tucked back, and our bellies scraped the pavement.

WHOOOSH! Suddenly, a huge cardboard box came tumbling down the sidewalk, carried by the wind.

"Whoa!" Pepperoni squeaked.

We all scuttled out of the way in the nick of time.

Next, an empty juice bottle rolled toward us. My brothers and I all leaped into the air, and the bottle rolled beneath our paws.

"This game is easy-cheesy, saucy-squeezy!" Veggie said.

His squeaks were cut off by another big *WHOOOOSH*. A shiny piece of paper blew our way.

I narrowed my eyes to see what it was. Could it be a candy wrapper? I gather those for my treasure collection.

But as the paper flew closer, I picked up a greasy scent that told me it was just a burger wrapper.

Veggie and Pepperoni scurried out of the way, but I was too late.

THWAP! The wrapper blew right into me, covering my face.

"Argh!" As I tried to pull the wrapper off my face, my brothers laughed.

"The game is called Dodge the Trash," Pepperoni said. "Not Get Smacked in the Face by Trash!"

Another burst of wind howled by. It swept the burger wrapper—and ME—right into the air!

The wind tossed me upside down and untangled me from the wrapper. For a moment, I was glad to be free.

But then I began falling straight toward the ground.

I somersaulted in the air, trying to get my feet below me. Somehow, I managed to land on my paws.

"Whoa!" Pepperoni and Veggie cheered. "You looked like a super rat!"

"Yeah," a mysterious voice chimed in. "A super DUPER rat!"

CHAPTER 2
EYE ON THE PRIZE

We swiveled our heads around, trying to find the mysterious voice. That's when I saw a bushy tail sticking out from behind a pole.

It was Ernie the squirrel!

"Hey, Ratnip," Ernie said. "You should really join the City Race tomorrow."

"The City Race?" I asked. "What's that?"

"It's a race through the city, with a bunch of obstacles in the way," Ernie explained. "If you win first place, you get a really big prize."

RATNIP FACT: I love collecting odds and ends from around The City. My siblings sometimes call me a hoarder. But I prefer to call myself a treasure hunter.

So any time I hear the word "prize," I only have one answer: YES!

It was time to launch . . .

OPERATION WIN THE CITY RACE!

Ernie led the way to the playground to begin my training. If the race was happening tomorrow, there was no time to lose.

First, he told me to run laps around the playground. The wind had calmed down a little, but I still had to work extra hard just to keep moving forward.

Pepperoni and Veggie thought it would be fun to train with me. But they felt silly running in circles like one of those humans who stayed up past their bedtime to run and jump around.

Me? I was willing to do silly things if it meant winning a special prize.

Next, Ernie drilled us through different exercises: ten push-ups, ten sit-ups, ten jumping jacks, and repeat.

Before long, Pepperoni's and Veggie's limbs gave out.

"No . . . more . . . please," they wheezed.

But I kept grinding through the exercises.

"The—prize—will—be—MINE!" I declared between each push-up.

Ernie wasn't impressed, though.

"If you really want to win the race," he said, "you've got to do a lot more than push-ups."

"What should I do?" I asked. Whatever it was, I was ready to do it!

"Follow me," Ernie replied, heading toward the playground's exit.

I turned around to wave goodbye to my brothers, who were still huffing and puffing. Then I scurried after Ernie, ready to start the next step in my training.

CHAPTER 3
GYM RATS

"Where are we going?" I asked Ernie, but he didn't answer. Either he couldn't hear me over the whooshing of the wind, or he wanted to keep me in suspense.

Ernie can be like that sometimes.

After a few blocks, we stopped in front of a fancy-looking building.

Ernie climbed up a streetlight, and I just kept following.

Soon we were as high as one of the building's open windows. I tried to peer in but couldn't see anything from this distance.

"Here we go!" Ernie said. He leaped straight through the open window and out of sight.

"Ernie?!" I yelled.

There was no answer.

Like I said, Ernie could be a little nutty. But this was the nuttiest thing I had ever seen him do!

Cookie, who takes care of my siblings and me, has always told me to never go inside a building that isn't our home.

I could hear Cookie's voice inside my head now: "Humans don't go into our houses, and we stay out of theirs."

But what if this was a test? What if I needed to make this jump through the window to win the City Race?

Another thing Cookie has always told me: "Give everything your best shot."

Well then, I was going to give this race my best shot. Even if it meant jumping through a window.

I took a deep breath. Then I pushed off the light pole, sailed through the open window . . . and landed on something super soft and squishy.

In the bright light, I could see Ernie standing next to two rats.

"Ratnip," he said, "meet Papa Flex and his kid, Pex."

RAT FACT: There are a lot of us rats living all around The City. So it's not too surprising when we run into each other.

But right away, I could tell Flex and Pex were no ordinary rats. They had perfect posture, with their shoulders squared and their chests puffed out. Their legs looked twice as thick as mine. Even their TAILS looked muscular.

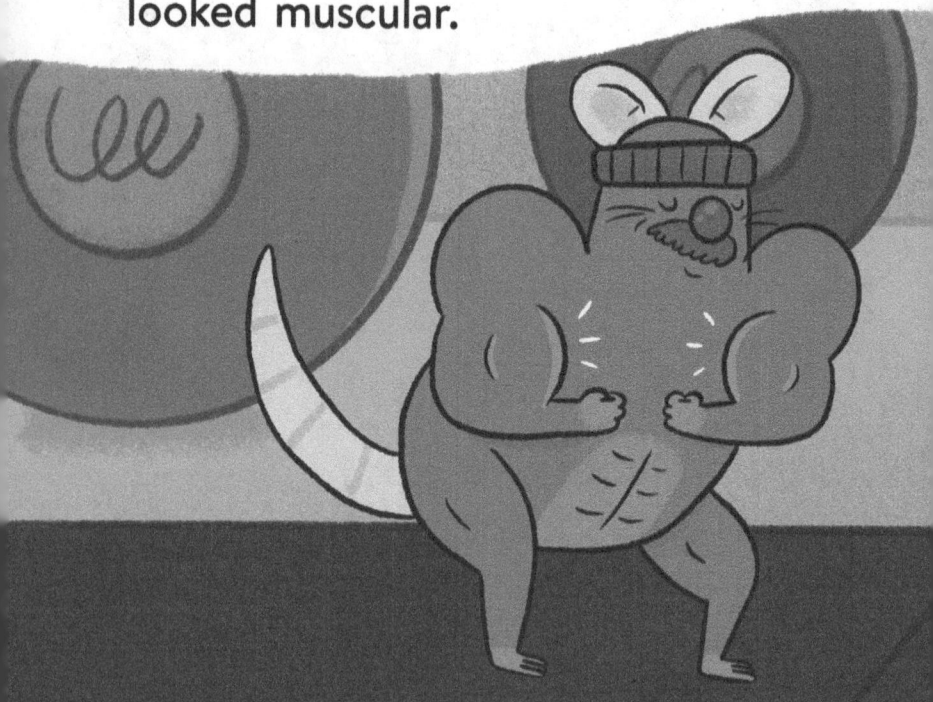

You might be wondering, how could a skinny rat tail look muscular?

Well, if you saw Flex and Pex, you would understand.

"Flex here has won the City Race five times," Ernie explained.

"That's right," Flex said. He led me over to a corner of the room. Inside a glass case, I saw five shiny, sparkly objects lined up in a row.

"Are these your trophies?" I gasped.

I had never seen anything like them before. They were all different shapes and sizes, and each one had a little chain connected to it.

I felt as if I'd been struck by lightning.

I really, REALLY wanted my own trophy!

"I've retired from racing," Flex continued. "But my daughter is running the City Race for the first time this year."

"That makes us rivals. Woo-hoo!" Pex said. She playfully punched me in the shoulder. But she was so strong, I nearly fell over!

"You came just in time. We're about to start our workout," Flex said. "Join us, Ratnip!"

Training with a former champion? Maybe Ernie wasn't so nutty after all.

This was my golden ticket to winning the City Race!

CHAPTER 4
NOT-SO-EASY WORKOUT

"What is this place?" I asked, looking around. There were all kinds of big machines. Some had buttons, others had stacks of metal plates.

"This is our home! It's called a gym," Pex answered. "During the day, humans exercise here. At night, we have the place all to ourselves."

"You'll get the full house tour during the workout," Flex said. "But first, let's stretch."

Flex and Pex stretched their paws up and down, then twisted to the right and to the left.

I copied their every move.

"Let's start with something nice and simple," Flex said, pointing to one of the machines.

Pex and I scampered onto the machine. I noticed it was made from some bouncy, rubber material I had never felt before.

Pex and I waited while her dad scurried all the way up to the top of the machine.

"Ready?" he called out.

"Ready!" Pex called back.

I, on the other hand, had no idea what I was supposed to be ready for!

From above my head, I heard a bunch of beeping noises from the machine.

Suddenly, the ground started moving under me!

"W-what's going on?!" I yelled.

"Just keep up," Pex replied as she jogged in place.

So I did as I was told. Even though I ran hard, I didn't even move a whisker's worth ahead.

It was the weirdest feeling ever.

After a while, I stopped to catch my breath. Turns out, that was a terrible idea.

I had stopped running, but the ground kept moving. I sailed backward and flew off the machine!

"AHHH!" I yelled, rocketing through the air. I bounced off another big, round, rubbery thing . . . and somehow landed right back where I had started.

"Whooooa," Pex said, impressed. "I've never landed that trick before."

But that was just the beginning of the workout. We scrambled up ropes. We swung from rings. We even wrapped our tails around a bar and hung upside down, just like bats.

Then we jumped and balanced on large, colorful balls. Well, I TRIED to balance.

All the while, Ernie lounged on the soft floor and ate pop-acorn, laughing every time I fell over.

Finally, at long last, the workout was over. My entire body felt wobbly like jelly.

Flex dragged me over to a giant water bottle. He pushed a lever, and I could feel the cool water running over me like a shower.

Ahhh. At least that felt nice.

"You both did well tonight," Flex said with his arms crossed. "But next time, I won't go so easy on you."

"Bring it on," Pex said, pumping her muscular arms in the air. "City Race, here we come!"

But I felt a shiver run down my spine.

EASY? That workout was supposed to be EASY?

CHAPTER 5
IN IT TO WIN IT

On the long walk home, my legs ached so much that I thought about quitting the race.

But then I remembered how fast news travels through The City.

First, Ernie would tell the other squirrels about me entering the race. Soon the pigeons would know too.

And by the time the alley cats started meowing . . . well, everyone would know.

My whole family was waiting for me at the front door.

"Welcome home, Ratnip the Racer!" they cheered.

See what I mean about news traveling fast? There was no way I could back out.

"Off to bed now," Cookie said. She nudged me over to my holey sock and practically stuffed me inside. "Racing rats need their rest!"

I was so tired from my workout with Pex and Flex, I fell asleep right away.

Before I knew it, the sun was setting outside. My sister Marg was shaking me awake. She wanted to help me train one more time before the race.

Marg timed me while I climbed up and down the fence behind our building. Then I used a piece of twine to jump rope. I even ran around the block while carrying my little sister, Anchovy, on my back.

Part of me wondered if I should be training again at Flex's and Pex's gym. But I didn't want to wipe myself out before the actual race.

Cookie, my sisters and brothers, and I headed out to the race. The night was clear and calm, with just a soft breeze.

Near the starting line, a pigeon was strutting around with a funny-looking machine tucked under her wing.

"Racers, step right up and take a number!" she called out.

I walked over and yanked on the little slip sticking out from the machine. It spit out a numbered ticket: 081.

Cool! I wished I could get one of these machines for my treasure collection.

I stuck the ticket onto my belly, just like I saw other racers doing.

A loud whistle quieted down the crowd. I turned toward the sound and saw Flex standing on top of the steps of a nearby building.

"As the champion of last year's City Race, I'm honored to unveil this year's trophy," he said.

He stepped aside and tugged on a rag that was covering a lump . . . revealing the biggest trophy I had ever seen.

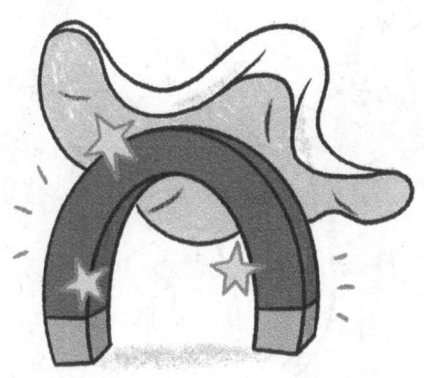

As it gleamed in the lamplight, my fur stood up like *ZING!*

Now I was so happy I didn't quit the race. In fact, I was super pumped.

I was in it to win it!

CHAPTER 6
THE RACE IS ON!

All kinds of critters were lined up at the starting line: raccoons and cats, squirrels and cockroaches, and, of course, rats. I joined them and started my warmup stretches.

Cookie and my siblings stood on the sidelines. They unrolled a big sign that said GO, RATNIP!

I smiled sheepishly and gave a little wave in return.

Suddenly, a paw slapped me on the back so hard, I started coughing.

"Ratnip! Can you believe race day is finally here?" Pex shouted. She had a ticket with the number 13 pinned to herself.

"Good luck," I said to her. "But that trophy is going to be MINE!"

"We'll see about that," she replied. This time, I knew to dodge to the side before she punched me in the arm again.

My heart went *thump-a-bump-bump* as more racers joined the starting line. There were so many. And if I was going to win, I would have to run faster and be stronger than all of them!

Over the noise of the crowd, Flex's voice boomed.

"Runners, take your marks, get set …"

I took a deep breath.

"GO!"

We all took off running down the sidewalk. The critters on the sidelines cheered as we passed.

"Aaaand the race has begun!" the pigeons tweeted from the sky.

They flew around in circles, keeping everyone up to date on the race.

"It's tail to tail, snout to snout, as the racers reach their first obstacle: the pole climb!"

For us rats, climbing a pole is no big deal. But the cockroaches kept slipping and sliding down. Their tiny feet didn't have enough grip to climb up.

"Hold on to my fur," I told the cockroaches. They grabbed on as I scurried up the pole.

Once we reached the top, the cockroaches jumped off my back.

"Thank you very much!" they said, bowing their antennae.

Next, the course took us across a set of tightropes strung high in the sky.

The raccoon in front of me set one paw onto the tightrope. It wobbled dangerously and sagged downward.

"This is so scary!" the raccoon whined, staring down at the ground far below. "I'm too big for this!"

"You can do it!" I tried to encourage him from behind, but Pex quickly leaped onto another tightrope to run right past us.

"Keep your eye on the prize!" she shouted at me.

Right, the prize! I leaped onto the other tightrope to follow Pex. Then I realized her message would be a good piece of advice for the raccoon too.

The raccoon was still shivering with fear as he peered down at the ground.

"Don't look down," I called out. "Just look up and keep your eye on the prize. You can do it!"

"Thanks!" The raccoon took a deep breath and nodded.

Once I saw that he was okay, I darted ahead and caught up to Pex. Together, we slid down a second pole. *Whee!*

When we landed on the sidewalk, it started raining out of nowhere. The sidewalk had turned into one big puddle!

Pex and I didn't miss a beat. We both jumped into the water and paddled across.

"The two rats have dived into the pool and are swimming their hearts out!" the birds tweeted from above.

Just as quickly as it started, the rain stopped. But I didn't have any time to wonder why, because the course continued between two buildings. There was just a tiny gap in between, barely large enough to fit a cockroach!

"Uh-oh!" the pigeons tweeted. "What is a rat to do?"

CHAPTER 7
RUN, RUN, RUN

RAT FACT: Rats are great at squeezing through very small openings.

Still, I have to admit, it's not exactly the prettiest sight.

But caring about our looks wasn't going to help us win the race. Pex and I flattened ourselves and shimmied between the two buildings.

Ahead of us, a tall gate of glass and metal blocked our path. There was no way we could climb up or go around it.

The only way forward was to push the gate open.

Racer number 62 was scratching away at the gate. She had already made a tiny opening, just big enough for us rats to squeeze through. But it certainly was not wide enough for a cat.

Pex darted past the cat and through the opening. But I couldn't just leave the cat in the dust.

"If we try together, we can open this gate," I said to the cat.

And so the cat and I pushed against the gate with all our might. "NRRRGGGGGH!"

Together, we heaved and shoved. Never before had I wished so hard for muscles like Pex and Flex had!

At last, we managed to get the gate open just wide enough for the cat and me to squeeze through.

"Thank you so much!" the cat said.

"Of course. I'll see you at the finish line!" I replied. Then I sprinted ahead to catch up with Pex.

"Racers, you're halfway through!" the crowd chanted.

I couldn't see any racers in front of us. All I had to do was outrun Pex before the finish line. And then the trophy would be mine!

Time for another RAT FACT: Not only can we squeeze through tiny openings, we also have excellent hearing. Sometimes, if I concentrate hard enough, I can hear someone unwrapping a cheeseburger from across the street!

That's how, over the noise of all the cheering, I heard a strange sound that didn't belong.

I perked my ears and listened hard. It almost sounded like . . . crying!

"Do you hear that?" I asked Pex.

"Hear what?" she answered. "The only sound I hear is the sound of my victory!"

I cocked my head. It sounded like the crying was coming from behind me.

I looked forward again to see where Pex was running a few steps ahead of me.

I wasn't sure what to do. If I wanted to win the prize, I'd have to stay right on Pex's tail.

But I just couldn't ignore the crying. What if someone needed help?

I took a deep breath, turned around, and ran back the way I'd come, letting my ears guide the way.

CHAPTER 8
WRONG WAY

"Hey, you're going the wrong way!" the critters standing on the sidelines yelled at me.

I ignored them and continued sprinting. I made it back to the metal gate, where I slipped through and ran ALL the way back to the tiny opening between the two buildings.

There, I came face to face with a squirrel. His furry face was covered in tears.

It was always a little surprising to see a squirrel at night. They're usually awake and busy during the day. (Well, except for Ernie, who never seems to sleep.)

But what was even more surprising was that this squirrel didn't have a body. He was just a floating head.

After a second, I realized I could only see the squirrel's head, which was peeking out from the tiny opening. The rest of his body was stuck between the buildings!

I could hear the pigeons tweeting above, describing how the other racers behind the squirrel were trying to push him from behind.

But the harder they pushed, the more stuck the squirrel got.

"In all our years covering the City Race, we've never seen anything like it!" the pigeons chirruped.

"What's your name?" I asked the squirrel head.

"Peanut," he replied between sobs.

"Well, don't worry, Peanut," I said. "I'm going to help you. Can you get one of your arms out?"

"I think so," Peanut said, sniffling.

He managed to wrestle one of his arms free. I grabbed his paw tight. Then I pulled and pulled, while the other racers pushed and pushed from behind.

Finally, with one great big yank, the rest of Peanut popped out from between the buildings. We both went flying!

We crashed down in a heap of legs and tails as the other racers zipped past us at top speed.

"Hooray, you're unstuck!" I cheered. But then I noticed Peanut was still upset.

"I think I twisted my tail," he said.

Oh no! I untied the bandana around my neck and refastened it around Peanut's tail like a sling.

"Can you still run?" I asked Peanut. "The other racers aren't too far ahead. We can catch up now!"

"You should go ahead without me," Peanut said, shaking his head.

But of course, I wasn't about to leave a hurt squirrel alone.

"It's okay," I said. "I'll stay with you."

Slowly, we hobbled along the sidewalk together, with Peanut leaning on me for support.

"Hooray for teamwork!" the birds tweeted. "That rat is taking one for the team!"

But I couldn't help but wonder: Would teamwork be enough to get through the final obstacle?

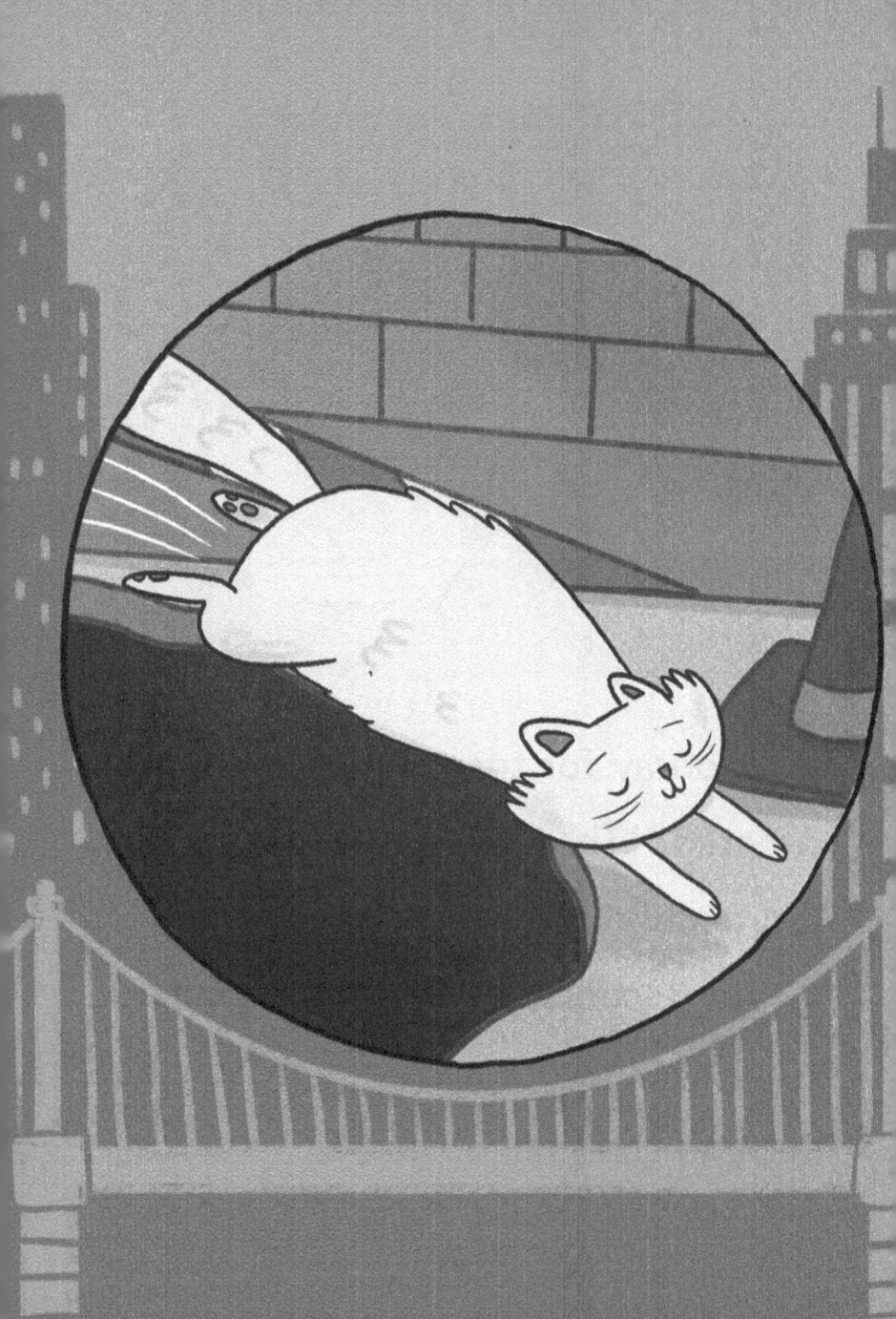

CHAPTER 9
THE FINAL OBSTACLE

Finally, we reached the last obstacle. The grand finale. The only thing standing between us and the goal.

It was a big, gaping hole in the ground.

The large critters leaped across it. Smaller animals inched along a tiny space between the pit and the wall.

But I wasn't sure if Peanut, with his wounded tail, would be able to do either of those things. He couldn't hurt his tail more than it already was.

As we stood there wondering what to do, more and more racers dashed past us.

"Almost there, Ratnip!" my family yelled from the sidelines.

I glanced over at Cookie and my siblings. The GO, RATNIP! banner billowed in a gust of wind.

"I've got it! The WIND!" I shouted.

I ran to the sidelines and took the banner from my family's paws. "I need to borrow this, just for a second!"

I grasped on to one end of the sign, and I told Peanut to hold on to the other.

"On the count of three, lift the banner high above your head," I instructed him. "One . . . two . . . three!"

WHOOOOOOSH! The wind picked us up and carried us off the ground. Just like it did yesterday with the burger wrapper and me.

"Wow!" The crowd gasped in awe as we drifted over the pit.

"My plan! It's working!" I shouted.

But in the next moment, the wind calmed down to a gentle breeze. I looked down with horror. We were headed straight INTO the pit!

"AHHHH!" Peanut and I screamed our heads off, and so did everyone on the sidelines.

Just when all hope seemed lost, we felt a sharp tug upward.

Something—no, SOMEONE—had grabbed onto the banner and was pulling us to safety!

"Goodness gracious!" the pigeons squawked from above. "The rat and squirrel are being rescued by a raccoon, some cockroaches, and . . . hold on a second . . . is that a cat?!"

Finally, my feet touched the ground again. Panting, I looked around at my rescuers.

I saw the cockroaches who had taken a ride on my back up the pole and the raccoon I had encouraged across the tightrope. And there was the cat with ticket number 62, who had pushed open the metal gate with me.

"Thank you," Peanut and I said to each and every one of them.

"You helped us, so now we help you," they all replied.

Peanut reached over and linked arms with me.

"Okay, let's all finish this race together!" he said.

So that is just what we did. A rat, cat, squirrel, raccoon, and a bunch of cockroaches crossed the finish line at the same time.

And together we shouted, "WE DID IT!"

CHAPTER 10
AND THE WINNER IS . . .

To no one's surprise, Pex won the City Race.

I found her in the crowd after the race. She was carrying her big, shiny trophy and wearing a giant grin on her face.

"Congratulations, Pex. You ran a good race," I said.

And I had to admit, I was sure the trophy would look really nice next to her dad's trophies, all sitting in the glass case.

"Thanks, Ratnip," Pex said, shaking my paw so hard I thought my arm might fall off. "You did a great job too."

Flex came over to us. His arms were overflowing with piles of food.

"Post-workout snack?" he asked, handing out a treat I'd never seen before.

YUM! I took a huge bite . . . and gagged.

"What is this?" I said, looking at the mysterious brown bar I had just shoved into my mouth.

"That is a protein bar," Flex explained. "You can find them everywhere in our gym."

"Mmm, it's SO yummy," Pex said, her cheeks full of protein bar.

My rat senses told me that these protein bars had something to do with why Flex and Pex were so strong and muscular.

But to me, the bars were so sticky and dry and chalky—all at the same time!

If this was the key to being a gym rat, I had one answer: No thank you!

I said goodbye to Pex and Flex.

I kept wandering through the crowd until I found my family. They all started talking excitedly at once.

"Ratnip, you looked so cool out there!" Anchovy said.

"Even when you were running backward," Veggie added, winking.

Pepperoni cleared his throat.

"We have something special for our very own rat racer," he said.

"You brought a gift?" I gasped. "For me?"

"We sure did!" Marg rooted around in her bag and pulled out something that gleamed in the lamplight.

It was a shiny golden bottle cap with a cord strung through a hole at the top. Cookie proudly placed it around my neck.

"This is your medal," she said. "You may not have won the race, but we are so proud of how you helped other racers in need."

"Thank you!" I said, beaming. Then I looked closer at the bottle cap. There were letters scratched onto it.

"MVR," I read aloud. "What does that mean?"

"Most Valuable Ratnip!" my siblings cheered in unison.

"You sure are the race's MVR!" Peanut said as he appeared next to me.

The raccoon, cat, and cockroaches were all standing nearby, smiling. I pulled them in for a big group hug.

I hadn't come close to winning the City Race trophy, but I wasn't bummed.

After all, I had finished my first ever City Race and made wonderful new friends. My family had given me a medal to add to my treasure collection. And most importantly, I had given it my best shot.

I couldn't wait to run the City Race again next year!

Here's a peek at Ratnip's next adventure!

RATNIP FACT: The City is one of the best places in the world.

The sidewalks are teeming with pecking pigeons, crawling cockroaches, and scurrying squirrels.

Not to mention the trash cans. They're always full of goodies, treasures, and snacks.

All of it waiting to be discovered by . . . me!

But The City isn't all candy wrappers and corndogs. There are some less than wonderful parts too.

Like the DUMPSTER MONSTER.

If you've never heard of this terrifying creature, you are not alone. I didn't know about it either until just the other night.

It was a warm evening. I was at the ice cream shop with my four siblings. Everywhere we looked, there were sweet ice cream puddles to slurp off the sidewalk.

And boy, did we slurp those puddles! Our whiskers and paws turned sticky, and our bellies filled up with sugary yumminess.

Once we had eaten our fill, we started heading back home. That's when I noticed a small alley behind the ice cream shop.